Falkirk
**Community
Trust**

Bo'ness
01506 778520
Bonnybridge
01324 503295
Denny
01324 504242
Falkirk
01324 503605
Grangemouth
01324 504690
Larbert
01324 503590
Meadowbank
01324 503870
Mobile
01324 506800
Slamannan
01324 851373

This book is due
for return on or
before the last date
indicated on the
label. Renewals
may be obtained
on application.

Falkirk Community Trust is a charity registered in Scotland. No: SC042403

2 9 MAR 2016

1 6 MAY 2016

2 0 JUL 2022

1 5 NOV 2016

- 6 DEC 2016

2 MAY 2017

2 4 JUL 2017

- 6 DEC 2021

1 6 AUG 2017

0 8 AUG 2018

CANCELLED

It was a **very** blustery day, and the wind had broken the swing. Charlie Brown put on his tool belt, determined to fix it.

He took out his hammer and nails . . .

"Duck!" shouted Charlie Brown over the sound of the wind. Springs and planks of wood hurtled towards Snoopy.

"It's no use, Snoopy," sighed Charlie Brown.
"Today is not a good day to fix the swing."

Charlie Brown called all his friends to tell them about the competition, then raced outside to practise with his kites.

It was always good to have more than one.

Charlie Brown had
just ONE kite left.
But it was his BEST one.

With a little gust, it took to the skies . . .

. . . and drifted **dangerously** close to a Kite-Eating Tree. *"Not again!"* said Charlie Brown, giving it a sharp tug. He hated Kite-Eating Trees.

It was time for the competition.
Sally arrived first.
"Hi, Sally!" smiled Charlie Brown, turning
round suddenly . . . and losing control of his kite.

Sally's kite took to the skies.
It flew **really** high and **really** fast.

Soon, everyone else
arrived with their kites.
"You can't enter the competition
without a kite, Charlie Brown," said Lucy.

The competition began and, before long, the sky was filled with colourful fluttering kites.

Meanwhile, Snoopy had built himself a
springboard. As Charlie Brown watched,
his crazy dog launched himself up
into the air . . .

As Snoopy flew past the Kite-Eating Tree, he made a grab for Charlie Brown's best kite.

Snoopy and the kite **soared** together across the sky!